STAR WARS™

MISSION 1

WRITTEN BY RAITH BLACK

HENDERSON
PUBLISHING LTD

There was nothing Princess Leia could do. Imperial stormtroopers had blasted their way on board the Rebel ship she was on. Directly behind the Imperial troops strode the sinister figure of Darth Vader. He was searching for secret plans of the Empire's ultimate weapon, the Death Star, which had been stolen. He believed the plans were on board this vessel.

In a corner of the ship, Princess Leia bent down to the droid, R2-D2, and gave him a message. She then slipped quietly away to try to hide from the Imperial troops.

Stormtroopers, searching the ship, later found Leia and brought her before Lord Vader.

"Where are those plans?" he asked menacingly.

"I don't know what you're talking about," Leia replied. Vader knew the princess was lying.

"Tear this ship apart until you've found those plans and bring me the passengers. I want them alive!"

C-3PO hurried behind R2-D2. Around them, the
Rebellion and the Empire were fighting fiercely
throughout the ship.

R2-D2 opened the hatch to an escape pod and
entered. C-3PO stood by the hatch – he wanted
to know why Artoo was in such a hurry to leave.
"Secret mission...what plans?" asked C-3PO,
after listening to his friend's beeps. At that
moment, blaster fire exploded into the wall
behind him, forcing him into the escape pod.
"I'm going to regret this," he complained, as the
door slid firmly shut behind him.

**Can you complete the sequence to
help Artoo release the escape pod?**

2, 5, 9, 14 ☐ ☐ ☐

When he learned of the escape pod, Lord Vader
was incensed. "She must have hidden the plans
on the escape pod. Send a detachment down to
retrieve them!"

C-3PO and R2-D2 landed in the dust and sand of planet Tatooine. Stumbling from the escape pod, they simply could not agree on which way to go. Artoo was still babbling about a mysterious secret mission. "You go that way," C-3PO said. "You won't find any settlements. This way is much easier." The droids walked away from one another. "And don't come looking to me for help," shouted C-3PO as he shuffled off alone.

It was not long before a party of stormtroopers arrived to search the area around the escape pod. One of them picked up a small piece of metal and held it up to his superior officer. "Look, sir," he said. "Droids!"

As R2-D2 approached the canyon, he failed to see the small Jawas. Keeping well out of sight, they waited until he drew nearer, then leaped out and disabled him. Tipping the poor droid on to his side, the Jawas stowed him in the back of their huge sandcrawler. A familiar voice rang out from inside. "Artoo? R2-D2 – it *is* you!" C-3PO had also been captured.

Which of the silhouettes matches the picture?

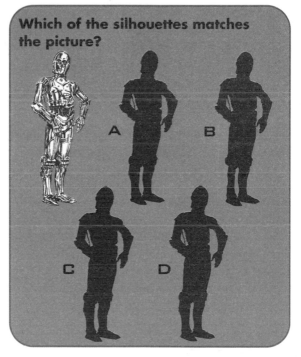

A

B

C

D

The Jawas soon sold the droids to Owen Lars, to be employed on his moisture farm. Owen was Luke Skywalker's uncle, and Luke was given the job of cleaning them. Working on the R2 unit, he dislodged something in the droid's casing. Luke stared in amazement as a hologram of a princess appeared in front of him.

"Help me, Obi-Wan Kenobi. You're my only hope." When the image faded, Luke asked Artoo to get it back. The droid beeped. "He claims he is the property of Obi-Wan Kenobi," explained C-3PO.

Called away, Luke returned to find that the pesky droid had gone missing. "He kept babbling on about his secret mission," stammered C-3PO, "and he's gone to look for Obi-Wan Kenobi."

"It's too dangerous to look for him now," said Luke. "We'll have to wait until morning."

Early the following morning, Luke and C-3PO set off in Luke's landspeeder to hunt for Artoo. Luke checked his scanner for readings.

"There's a droid on the scanner – dead ahead," he said. He drew closer and stopped to scan the area with his high-powered glasses. He could see movement down below – and it looked ominously like Sand People!

Suddenly, right in front of him, one appeared. Luke had no chance to get out of the way, and the creature knocked him unconscious. The Sand People soon gathered around Luke's landspeeder.

 A terrible howl split the air and scattered the crowds of Sand People. The hooded figure of a man approached and bent over Luke. He saw Artoo hiding, and beckoned the droid forward. "Come here my little friend, don't be afraid."

Luke woke up and recognised the man instantly. "Ben!" he said. "Am I glad to see you!"

Can you unscramble the words to find the name of the sand people?

EKUSNT RRDAIES

"This droid claims to be the property of Obi-Wan Kenobi," said Luke. "Do you know him?"

"Yes," said the man, "though it's a name I haven't heard in a long, long time. It's me. But I don't seem to remember owning a droid."

Obi-Wan took Luke into his home. He had to speak to him about his father. "He asked me to give you this when you were old enough." Luke watched as Obi-Wan took an object out of a box and handed it to him. "It's a lightsaber – the weapon of a Jedi Knight. Your father was a Jedi who was betrayed and murdered by Darth Vader. Vader was seduced by the dark side of the Force."

"The Force?" asked Luke uncertainly.

"It's an energy field which gives a Jedi Knight his power."

Artoo beeped impatiently, prompting Obi-Wan
to run the hologram message from the princess.
"Obi-Wan Kenobi, my father begs you to help
him in the struggle against the Empire. I have
placed information which is vital to the survival
of the Rebellion inside this R2 unit. My father will
know how to retrieve it. You must see this droid
safely to Alderaan. Help me, Obi-Wan Kenobi.
You're my only hope."
Obi-Wan turned portentously to Luke.
"You must learn the ways of the Force, Luke, if
you're to come with me to Alderaan."
"I can't go to Alderaan," said Luke. "It's too far.
Besides, I have work to do here – I can take you
to Anchorhead. From there you should be able
to get transport on to Mos Eisley."

Which of R2-D2's component parts is needed to produce the hologram?

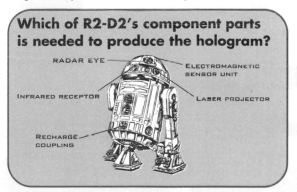

RADAR EYE

ELECTROMAGNETIC
SENSOR UNIT

INFRARED RECEPTOR

LASER PROJECTOR

RECHARGE
COUPLING

During their journey, they came across the Jawas' sandcrawler. It had been destroyed – but by what?

"These blast points are too accurate for Sand People," said Obi-Wan. "Only Imperial stormtroopers are so precise."

"But why would Imperial troops want to slaughter Jawas?" Luke asked. Then he realised – the droids. "If they traced the robots here they may have learned who they sold them to and that would lead them back...home!" He raced towards his landspeeder.

Obi-Wan tried to call him back. But Luke's mind was made up – he must reach home before it was too late.

He arrived to find that the Empire had beaten him to it. The farm, his home, his aunt and uncle – all mercilessly destroyed. He returned sorrowfully to Obi-Wan and the droids.

"There's nothing you could have done, Luke. If you had been there, the droids would now be in the hands of the Empire," said Ben reassuringly. Luke knew he was right. Thinking for a while, he made his decision. "I'm going to come with you to Alderaan. I want to learn the ways of the Force to become a Jedi like my father." Accompanied by the droids, Luke and Obi-Wan took the landspeeder to the cantina at the Mos Eisley Spaceport. Before they went in, Obi-Wan warned Luke about the dangers in the town. "Mos Eisley is…well, let me just say that you won't find a more wretched hive of scum and villainy. We must be cautious, Luke, but we will find a pilot who can take us to Alderaan."

Starting at the coloured spot, travel along the lines of the grid to spell out the name of Obi-Wan's weapon. You must not cross any letter or line more than once.

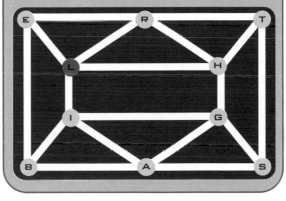

A bizarre band was playing in the cantina. It was a rough place filled with strange aliens, most of them thugs and villains. Obi-Wan and Luke were introduced to a man and a huge, furry creature called a Wookiee. "I'm Han Solo, captain of the *Millennium Falcon*," said the man. He pointed to the Wookiee. "This is my co-pilot, Chewbacca. My ship is fast. She'll take you where you want to go. What's the cargo?" Obi-Wan spoke. "Only passengers. Myself, the boy, two droids and no questions. I'll pay 2,000 now and another 15,000 when we get to Alderaan." Han raised his eyebrows. "17,000? Got yourself a little local trouble, eh?"

"I'd just like to avoid any Imperial entanglement." Han nodded knowingly. "We'll leave as soon as you're ready. Docking Bay 94."

bi-Wan, Luke and the droids headed quickly to the docking bay. Behind them, unseen, a shadowy silhouette followed. They entered the docking bay, and the figure spoke into a comlink, alerting Imperial troops to the whereabouts of Luke and the droids.

Luke was unimpressed with the *Millennium Falcon*. "What a piece of junk!"

"She may not look like much, but she's got it where it counts, kid." Suddenly, from behind them, Imperial stormtroopers burst into the bay and started firing. Han turned on them, returning fire with his blaster. "Get on board and we'll get out of here!" he yelled.

"Stop that ship!" ordered one of the stormtroopers. Under fire, Han rushed everyone on board and took off. With a powerful roar, the *Falcon* flew away from the docking bay.

The word '*Millennium*' appears twice in this grid. Can you spot it both times?

L	I	M	N	M	E	L	L	I	M
M	U	I	N	N	E	L	L	I	M
I	E	L	I	M	I	L	L	E	L
L	I	L	I	N	E	M	L	I	I
M	I	L	L	E	N	N	I	U	M
I	L	I	I	I	I	I	N	I	I
E	N	M	I	L	M	N	L	N	L

The *Falcon* quickly came under fire from two Imperial destroyers. The ship shuddered with the force of the attack.

"We'll be safe enough once we make the jump to hyperspace," Han said, operating the controls.

"I thought you said this thing was fast!" Luke snapped.

"Travelling through hyperspace ain't like dusting crops, boy. It has to be precise."

Luke was thrown back against his seat as the *Millennium Falcon* suddenly gathered speed and jumped into hyperspace. The view through the window was a blur of rushing stars.

Han has a secret number to select lightspeed. It is the number of squares in this picture. How many are there?

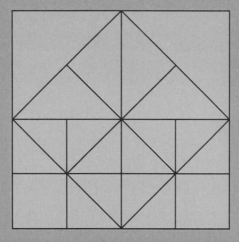

O n board the Death Star, Grand Moff Tarkin and Darth Vader were holding Princess Leia prisoner. It seemed that none of their methods would convince her to reveal the information they wanted.

"Since you are reluctant to provide us with the location of the Rebel base, I have chosen to test this space station's destructive power on your home planet of Alderaan."

"No!" cried Leia. "It's a peaceful planet. We have no weapons."

"Then give me a military target," threatened Tarkin menacingly.

Leia bowed her head. "Dantooine," she whispered.

To Leia's horror, Tarkin ordered the destruction of Alderaan anyway. "Dantooine is too remote for an effective demonstration of this station's power, but we'll deal with your Rebel friends soon enough."

Leia was forced to watch as an immense and powerful beam of energy blasted from the Death Star, fragmenting Alderaan into millions of tiny pieces.

O bi-Wan was on the *Millennium Falcon*, trying to teach Luke about the Force, when he sensed the destruction of Alderaan. "I felt a great disturbance in the Force," he whispered. "It was as if millions of voices suddenly cried out in terror and were silenced."

He took a while to compose himself, then resumed his teaching. He placed a helmet over Luke's head to blindfold him. Luke held the lightsaber in his hand.

"Trust your feelings, Luke. Feel the Force." A remote shot lasers at Luke. Using the Force, he parried each shot with the aid of his lightsaber. At that moment Han interrupted the lesson.

"We're approaching Alderaan."

Luke, Han, Obi-Wan and Chewie were on the flight deck when the ship entered the area that was formerly Alderaan. They found themselves instead in an asteroid field.

Han was puzzled. "This is the correct place," he said, "but Alderaan ain't there."

Suddenly, an Imperial TIE fighter appeared and fired at the *Falcon*. Han took chase.

"A fighter that size couldn't get this deep into space on its own," said Obi-Wan. "It's a short range fighter."

"If it recognises us, we're in trouble," Luke added.

Han tried to jam its transmission.

"Look — it's heading for that small moon," pointed Luke.

In the distance, the small moon became closer. Obi-Wan realised immediately what it was. "That's no moon," he informed them knowledgeably. "That's a space station. Quick. Turn this thing around."

Han tried, but the *Falcon* juddered and shook. "I can't! We're caught in a tractor beam." Slowly, the space station pulled the *Millennium Falcon* closer and closer.

What can Han do next to save the *Millennium Falcon*? Can you work it out from the code?
Clue: A = 26   B = 25   C = 24   D = 23

8 - 19 - 6 - 7
23 - 12 - 4 - 13
11 - 12 - 4 - 22 - 9

nside the space station, the *Millennium Falcon* was thoroughly searched. The Imperial stormtroopers were disappointed to find it empty. Darth Vader approached.

"Search again!" he demanded. Then he paused. "I sense something – a presence I have not felt since…" Disturbed by his feelings, he turned suddenly and walked away from the ship.

Once the coast was clear, Han and the others emerged from their hiding places in the *Millennium Falcon*. They had squeezed themselves into compartments which Han used for smuggling.

"I never thought I'd be smuggling myself," he remarked wryly. He wondered how they were going to escape from the Death Star. "Even if we could take off," he said, "we'd never get past the tractor beam."

"Leave that to me," said Obi-Wan. "I'll deactivate the tractor beam."

Wasting no time, Han and Luke overpowered two stormtroopers and slipped on their uniforms. Confident in disguise, they made their way to a control room and walked in. Artoo plugged in to the computer and Threepio translated his bleeps. "He says he's found the controls to the power beam that's holding the ship here. He'll try to make the precise location appear on the screen." "I'll go alone," said Obi-Wan, studying the monitor. "You stay here, Luke. Your destiny lies along a different path from mine."

Can you help Obi-Wan find his way to the power supply?

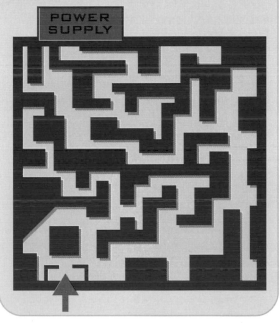

POWER SUPPLY

When Obi-Wan had gone, Artoo made a startling discovery. He began to beep excitedly. C-3PO explained. "He says 'I've found her,' and keeps saying she's here…"

"Who?" asked Luke.

"Princess Leia. She's in the detention cells and she's scheduled to be terminated."

"We must save her!" said Luke.

Han wasn't so sure – all he wanted was to get off the Death Star…fast! But Luke promised him he would be a rich man if he saved the princess, and this was enough to tempt him to stay.

Luke had an idea. He tried to place handcuffs on Chewie, but the Wookiee roared and pushed him away. Han took the cuffs from Luke and placed them on his friend.

"Don't worry, Chewie. I think I know what he has in mind."

What is the least number of doors the party must go through to reach the detention centre?

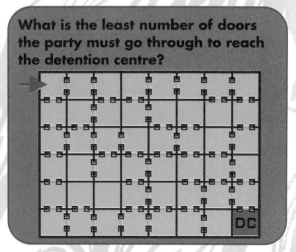

With Chewie in chains, Luke and Han escorted him to the detention centre. One of the guards there questioned their arrival.

"Prisoner transfer," explained Han, shrugging his shoulders.

"I wasn't notified," said the guard suspiciously. "I'll have to clear it." When the guard picked up the comlink, Han handed Chewie a blaster.

"Watch out!" Han yelled. "He's loose!"

A fight broke out. Han, Luke and Chewie soon had control of the detention centre. Hastily, Luke went to find Leia.

A stormtrooper called up the detention centre and asked what was going on. "Just a little trouble, that's all," explained Han.

"Who is this?" asked the guard. "What's your number?" Han didn't reply, choosing instead to destroy the desk with his blaster. He knew it would cause trouble.

"Luke!" he yelled. "Prepare yourself for company!"

Luke has found Leia's cell, but the door is coded. He must select one number from each pair so that they add together to make 100. Which figure from each pair must he choose?

19	12		16	27		41	42
30	17		13	11		ENTER	

"**Y**ou're a little short for a stormtrooper," Leia remarked when Luke entered her cell.

"I'm here to rescue you," said Luke. "I've come with Ben Kenobi."

She jumped up excitedly at the Jedi's name. "Ben Kenobi – where is he?" Just then, a commotion grabbed their attention. Stormtroopers began pouring into the detention centre. Han and Chewie were backing up the corridor, firing at the troops.

Soon, they were all trapped. Han and Luke ducked behind the supports, blasting down towards the stormtroopers.

"This is some rescue!" Leia remarked sarcastically. She grabbed Han's blaster and blew a hole in the wall, revealing a chute.

"What do you think you're doing?" Han asked.

"Somebody has to save our skins," Leia replied. "Now into the garbage chute, fly boy!" One by one, they all dived into the chute.

The chute ended in a mass of garbage. They were all up to their knees in filthy water. Han fired his blaster towards the door. The shot ricocheted around the walls.

"Put that thing away!" yelled Leia angrily, "before you get us all killed."

"There's something alive in here," Luke remarked with alarm. The water was churning slightly.

"I've got a bad feeling about this," said Han.

Out of the blue, something grabbed Luke's leg and pulled him under. The others tried to catch him, but he was gone.

Suddenly, he shot back up to the surface, choking and spluttering. There was silence for a moment, then the walls creaked and began to move. They started to slide together.

"Don't just stand there, try and brace it with something!" Leia shouted.

Luke tried to contact C-3PO on the comlink, but there was no response.

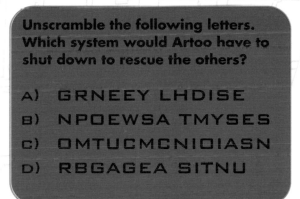

Unscramble the following letters. Which system would Artoo have to shut down to rescue the others?

A) GRNEEY LHDISE

B) NPOEWSA TMYSES

C) OMTUCMCNIOIASN

D) RBGAGEA SITNU

The two droids made their way back to the *Millennium Falcon*, avoiding the stormtroopers who milled around everywhere. C-3PO was concerned to find that the others were not on board. "Where could they be?" he asked aloud.

Artoo connected into the Death Star's computer and then blipped and whirred. C-3PO did as he was told and switched on the comlink. As soon as it was activated, he heard Luke's voice screaming at him.

"Are you there, sir?" C-3PO asked.

Luke was delighted to hear from C-3PO. "Shut down all the garbage mashers on the detention level," he yelled.

"Shut them all down, hurry!" C-3PO shouted to Artoo. The droid found the correct system and shut it down.

Over the comlink, C-3PO heard Luke and the others whooping with delight as the walls stopped closing in.

n a circular ledge in the centre of a high room, Obi-Wan found the power supply to the tractor beam. He shuffled around the ledge and pulled down on the switch. The power level drained off, shutting down the beam. A group of stormtroopers appeared at the entrance. They split up, leaving two on guard. Obi-Wan distracted their attention, and hastily made his escape.

Whilst Obi-Wan is busy, Luke and the others must open up the garbage unit to get out. What sequence of shapes should Luke press?

○ △ □ △ ○ △ ☐ ☐ ○ △ □ △

F inding their way out of the garbage unit, Luke and the others arrived at a window overlooking the *Millennium Falcon*. The ship was heavily guarded.

Leia pointed to the ship. "You came in *that?*" she mocked. "You're braver than I thought."

As they rounded a corner, they came face to face with a group of stormtroopers. Han chased after them, firing his blaster.

"He certainly has courage," Leia remarked.

Suddenly, Han skidded to a stop. He was staring at a blockade of stormtroopers. Time to retreat! A large blast door was closing. Han leaped towards it and, by the skin of his teeth, he managed to dive through the gap as it closed.

Luke and Leia stepped through a door and closed it behind them. They found themselves on a high plateau overlooking a bottomless drop. "I think we took a wrong turn!" said Luke.

Above them, a group of stormtroopers started firing at them. Luke handed his blaster to Leia. She fired back, pinning the stormtroopers down.

Behind them, another set of troopers began to ease open the door.

Luke removed a grappling hook and a rope from his belt. He swung it around his head and the hook caught hold. Leia held on to him and kissed his cheek.

"For luck."

Together, they swung across the chasm, landing safely on the opposite side.

Rearrange the letters to spell out a saying.

HET AYM EB OYU ERCFO THWI

Darth Vader watched as the figure of Obi-Wan approached. The red blade of his lightsaber buzzed at his side, ready to duel.

"I've been waiting for you, Obi-Wan. We meet again at last. The circle is now complete. When I left, I was the learner. Now I am the master."

Obi-Wan flicked his lightsaber into life. "Only the master of evil, Darth."

Vader stepped forward to attack. The air crackled with energy as the two lightsabers made contact, sparking loudly with the force of the blows.

Obi-Wan fought off the blows. "If you strike me down, Vader, I shall become more powerful than you can ever imagine."

uke and the others stood out of sight near the *Millennium Falcon*, wondering how they could get past the armed guards. At that moment, they watched in amazement as, suddenly, the guards started to move away from the ship. Taking his chance, Han ran towards the *Falcon*, with Luke, Leia, Chewie and the droids in hot pursuit.

> **Unscramble all the names and write down the odd letter left from each anagram. Rearrange these leftover letters to make another name.**
>
> **BWOIENA**
> **VDRATDRWAEH**
> **KSYWKLLEKRHAUE**
> **NOLISOAH**
> **KCNMFOFRTAI**
> **AESPIELENCRSI**

As he ran across the hangar floor, Luke saw what had attracted the attention of the guards. Obi-Wan was fighting with Vader.
He stopped running. "Ben?" he said.
Obi-Wan turned to look at Luke. He knew what he had to do – he raised his lightsaber in front of him and stood still.

Seeing his chance, Vader sliced his lightsaber
through Obi-Wan with one fatal blow.
"NO!" Luke screamed.
The stormtroopers turned and started firing.
Luke, filled with rage at the death of Obi-Wan,
fired back.
Darth Vader felt Obi-Wan's cloak. It was empty.
Obi-Wan had disappeared.
Luke then heard Obi-Wan's voice call to him.
"Run, Luke!" Luke obeyed, and started running
towards the *Falcon*.
Han shouted at him. "Blast the door, kid!"
Turning, Luke fired at the main control panel to
the hangar door. The door slid shut, sealing off
the stormtroopers.

nside the *Millennium Falcon*, Han moved fast to power up the engines.

"I hope the old man got that tractor beam out of commission, or this is gonna be a real short trip."

The *Falcon* blasted out of the Death Star and into space. Luke slumped on a chair, wretched at the loss of Obi-Wan. Leia placed a blanket over his shoulders to comfort him.

"I can't believe he's gone," Luke sighed.

Han appeared. "Come on," he warned. "We're not out of this yet."

Luke jumped up from his seat and took up position on one of the cannons. Han manned the other one. In the distance, Luke could see a group of Imperial TIE fighters approaching. He prepared himself to defend the *Millennium Falcon*.

How many TIE fighters are there?

$$8 \times 2 + 4 \div$$

$$5 \times 1 = ?$$

"Okay, kid," Han said, "stay sharp!"

"Here they come," informed Leia tensely.

The fighters swooped down on the *Falcon* from different directions, screaming as they attacked. Luke and Han fired the cannons hard. The fighters were difficult to hit.

"They're coming in too fast!" Luke yelled.

One by one, they managed to pick the fighters off. Han destroyed one first, then Luke.

"I got one!" Luke bellowed excitedly.

Han calmed him down. "Great, kid! Don't get cocky..." The *Falcon* took a strike. She shuddered with the impact.

Luke blasted furiously at one of the fighters and was delighted to see his shots hit home.

Han attacked the last fighter. It exploded in a huge fireball in front of him.

"We did it!" Luke exclaimed with relief.

Han wasted no time, and escaped before more fighters appeared. He made the jump to lightspeed.

W atching the fight with interest from the Death Star were Moff Tarkin and Darth Vader.

"Are they away?" Tarkin asked.

"They've just made the jump into hyperspace," said Vader.

"You're sure the homing beacon is secure aboard their ship?"

"Yes," replied Vader. He was extremely pleased. The homing beacon on board the *Millennium Falcon* would lead him directly to the Rebel base. Soon he would be able to destroy the Rebel Alliance – forever.

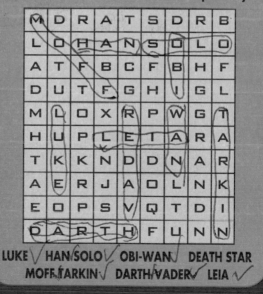

Can you find the words in the grid below? Hunt for each word in the names separately.

M	D	R	A	T	S	D	R	B
L	O	H	A	N	S	O	L	O
A	T	F	B	C	F	B	H	F
D	U	T	F	G	H	I	G	L
M	L	O	X	R	P	W	G	T
H	U	P	L	E	I	A	R	A
T	K	K	N	D	D	N	A	R
A	E	R	J	A	O	L	N	K
E	O	P	S	V	Q	T	D	I
D	A	R	T	H	F	U	N	N

LUKE HAN SOLO OBI-WAN DEATH STAR
MOFF TARKIN DARTH VADER LEIA

O n one of the moons orbiting the planet Yavin, the Rebel Alliance held a briefing before attacking the Death Star. The plans for the space station, retrieved from R2-D2, were displayed on a screen. The Rebel leader told the pilots what they had to do. "The battle station is heavily shielded. It has been designed to defend against a large scale assault, but it has a weakness. A small fighter is required to fly down a trench to a target two metres wide. The target is a thermal exhaust. A precise hit with proton torpedoes will set off a chain reaction which will destroy the space station… Man your ships. May the Force be with you."

The Death Star approached the planet Yavin. The homing beacon placed on board the *Millennium Falcon* had led Vader to this location. He watched the screen as the planet grew closer.

He turned to Moff Tarkin and spoke. "Today is a historic day. It has seen the end of Obi-Wan Kenobi and soon it will see the end of the Rebellion."

Han decided to leave before the attack. He was loading the *Millennium Falcon* when Luke approached him. Luke was wearing the uniform of a Rebel pilot and was about to join the attack on the Death Star.

"We could use a good pilot like you, Han, why don't you stay?"

Han was determined to leave. "I have debts to pay, kid. Sorry. Besides, attacking a space station sounds more like suicide." Luke became angry. He couldn't believe that Han was planning to leave them in their hour of need.

"Well, take care of yourself, Han. I guess that's what you're best at!" Sulkily, he walked away. Han called back, "Hey, Luke. May the Force be with you." Luke smiled weakly, wishing that Han would change his mind.

Chewie felt the same way. The Wookiee growled at Han. He believed they should stay and fight.

"What are you looking at?" snapped Han. "I know what I'm doing."

The X-wing fighters approached the formidable Death Star in formation. The voice of Obi-Wan comforted Luke. "Luke. The Force will be with you." The lead pilot issued his command. "Accelerate to attack speed." The wings of the fighters opened to assume their familiar X-wing shape. The pilots sped towards their destiny.

"Look at the size of that thing!" exclaimed one of the pilots in disbelief.

The Death Star continued its course towards Yavin. It would only be a matter of time until the Rebel base came into view and it could be destroyed.

The X-wings attacked. The huge cannons on the Death Star fired at the fighters, blasting some of them out of space. The pilots used all their skill and judgement to manoeuvre their small ships between the cannons and into the trenches.

Shade in the boxes as directed. The remaining letters should spell something very much on Darth Vader's mind at the moment.

	A	B	C	D
1	Y	X	R	P
2	S	A	W	O
3	V	M	I	F
4	B	C	T	N

Shade in:
1B, 2C, 4A, 3D, 2D, 4B, 2A, 1C, 3B, 4C, 1D

Darth Vader was informed of the success of the Rebel pilots. Most of them had managed to evade the main defences and were flying inside the trenches of the space station.

Vader decided to use the Imperial fighters. "We'll have to destroy them ship to ship. Get the crews to their fighters." The X-wings headed directly towards their target. The pilots flew through narrow gaps and swerved to avoid the cannon fire.

Soon, enemy fighters appeared and attacked from the rear. The TIE fighters swooped down from above and tailed the Rebel pilots. They fired their weapons accurately, blasting some of the X-wings, sending them crashing into the structure of the space station.

Luke heard Obi-Wan's voice, calming and instructing him. "Luke, trust your feelings."

Realising that the Rebel pilots were a danger to the station, Vader instructed a group of Imperial fighter pilots to follow him. He decided to fly his own fighter in order to destroy the Rebels. Luke tried to shake off his own shadow. He swerved from side to side, but the TIE fighter stayed on his tail. Just as the TIE was about to fire at Luke, one of the Rebel pilots flew in from the rear and blasted it into the side of the trench. Darth Vader guided his fighter into the trench. "Stay in attack formation," he ordered.

One of the Rebel pilots approached the target, releasing his torpedoes. They slammed into the side of the exhaust port. "I missed!" he said. This was Luke's cue – he swooped in to approach the target. Vader tailed him. Using every bit of skill he had, Luke flew through the trench. The walls closed in on either side. Behind him, Darth Vader fired, blasting Artoo's dome. "I've lost Artoo!" Luke yelled.

Back on the moon of Yavin, C-3PO sighed. He hoped his little friend would be all right.
Obi-Wan's voice instructed Luke. "Use the Force, Luke. Let go."
"The Force is strong with this one," Darth Vader remarked. He was closing in on Luke.
"Luke, trust me," said Obi-Wan.
Luke obeyed Obi-Wan and allowed the strength of the Force to flow through him. He switched off his targeting computer.

Which of the targets should Luke fire at? It is directly below two TIE fighters, but there are no X-wings next to it. It has a TIE bomber directly to its left.

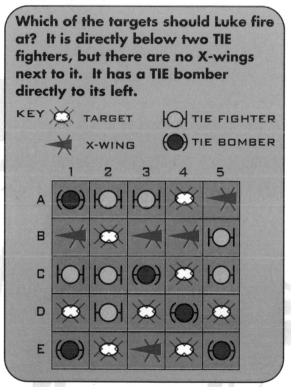

"I'm okay," assured Luke to the Rebel base. He tuned in to the Force and the target appeared. Luke prepared to fire.

On his tail, Darth Vader manoeuvred his fighter and locked Luke in his sights. "I have you now," he hissed.

Suddenly, a shot from above slammed into Vader's fighter. He spun out of the trench and into space.

Luke was delighted to hear Han's familiar voice burst over the comlink. So he had decided to stay and fight after all…and luckily for Luke he had arrived at just the right moment to blast Vader's fighter.

"It's all clear, kid. Now let's blow this thing and go home."

The Death Star had the Rebel base within range. Moff Tarkin ordered its destruction.

Luke concentrated on his target. Using the Force, he released two proton torpedoes, timing it just right. They hit the target and flew down the shaft. Sweeping his fighter out of the trench, Luke flew at full speed away from the Death Star. Behind him, the chain reaction started and the space station exploded in a huge fireball. Luke's mission had been successful.

D arth Vader sat helpless as his fighter spun wildly into space. Through the window, he could see the explosion which had destroyed the Death Star.

Obi-Wan spoke to Luke as he returned to the Rebel base.

"Remember, Luke. The Force will be with you always."

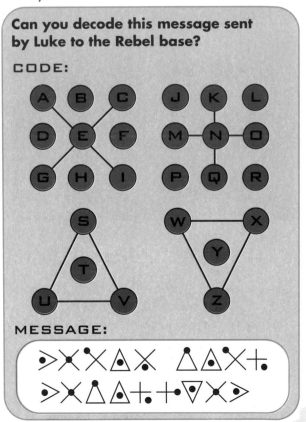

Can you decode this message sent by Luke to the Rebel base?

CODE:

MESSAGE:

On the Rebel base, the Alliance held a ceremony to honour the battle heroes. Luke, Han and Chewie walked proudly between rows of Rebel fighters to receive their awards. On the platform, Princess Leia welcomed them and presented them all with medals for bravery. R2-D2, who had been repaired, and C-3PO watched from the side. Once the medals were presented, all the people cheered and applauded. Luke, Han and the others had saved them all from the clutches of the evil Empire.

ANSWERS

Page 3 20, 27, 35
Page 5 C
Page 7 Tusken Raiders
Page 9 The laser projector is needed to produce the hologram.
Page 11 Obi-Wan's weapon is a lightsaber.

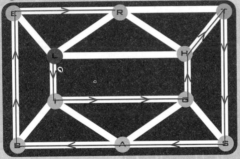

Page 13

L	I	M	N	M	E	L	L	I	M
~~M~~	~~U~~	~~I~~	~~N~~	~~N~~	~~E~~	~~L~~	~~L~~	~~I~~	~~M~~
I	E	L	I	M	I	L	L	E	L
L	I	L	I	N	E	M	L	I	I
~~M~~	~~I~~	~~L~~	~~L~~	~~E~~	~~N~~	~~N~~	~~I~~	~~U~~	~~M~~
I	L	I	I	I	I	I	N	I	I
E	N	M	I	L	M	N	L	N	L

POWER SUPPLY

Page 27 May the
Force be with you.
Page 29 Obi-Wan
Darth Vader
Luke Skywalker
Han Solo
Moff Tarkin
Princess Leia
The leftover letters
spell *Chewie.*
Page 31 4
Page 33

M	D	R	A	T	S	D	R	B
L	O	H	A	N	S	O	L	O
A	T	F	B	C	F	B	H	F
D	U	T	F	G	H	I	G	L
M	L	O	X	R	P	W	G	T
H	U	P	L	E	I	A	R	A
T	K	K	N	D	D	N	A	R
A	E	R	J	A	O	L	N	K
E	O	P	S	V	Q	T	D	I
D	A	R	T	H	F	U	N	N

Page 38 Yavin
Page 41 D5
Page 44 Death Star
destroyed